MW00973433

PowerKids Readers:
Nature Books™

Oceans

Kristin Ward

The Rosen Publishing Group's
PowerKids Press™
New York

For Thomas and Mak, with love.

Published in 2000 by The Rosen Publishing Group, Inc.
29 East 21st Street, New York, NY 10010

Copyright © 2000 by The Rosen Publishing Group, Inc.

All rights reserved. No part of this book may be reproduced in any form without permission in writing from the publisher, except by a reviewer.

First Edition

Book design: Michael de Guzman

Photo Credits: pp. 1, 13 © Telegraph Colour Library/FPG International; p. 5 © 1996 Andromeda Interactive Ltd.; pp. 7, 17 © Wayne Aldridge/International Stock; p. 9 © 1995 Digital Stock; p. 11 © Gail Shumway/FPG International; p. 14 © David Fleetham/FPG International; p. 15 CORBIS/Jeffrey L. Rotman; p. 19 CORBIS/Galen Rowell; p. 21 © Steve Easton/International Stock.

Ward, Kristin.
    Oceans / by Kristin Ward.
    p. cm. — (Nature books)
    Includes index.
    SUMMARY: Describes what oceans are and who lives in them.
    ISBN: 0-8239-5532-X (lib. bdg.)
    1. Oceans—Juvenile literature. [1. Ocean life. 2. Oceans.] I. Title. II.
Series: Nature books (New York, N.Y.)
    QL77.5 W359 1999
    636.088'9—dc21
                                                    98-49733
                                                       CIP
                                                        AC

Manufactured in the United States of America

Contents

The water that covers
most of the earth is called
the ocean.

5

Ocean water is saltwater.

There are many fish in the ocean. Sharks live in the ocean.

9

Big animals live in the ocean, too. Dolphins live in the ocean.

The biggest animal in the world lives in the ocean. This animal is the blue whale.

13

Some animals live at the
bottom of the ocean.
Shrimps and lobsters live
at the bottom of the
ocean.

15

Lots of plants live in the ocean. Seaweed is a plant that lives in or near the ocean.

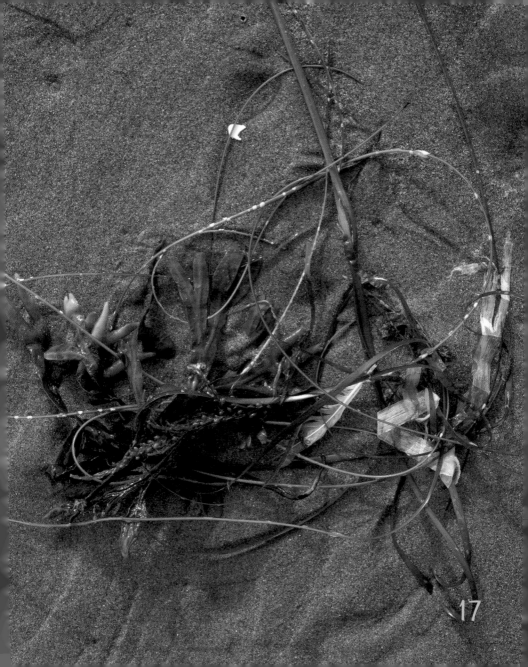

17

People like the ocean,
too. People ride in big
boats on the ocean.

19

Many families like to swim in the ocean.

Words to Know

BLUE WHALE

BOAT

DOLPHIN

LOBSTER

OCEAN

SEAWEED

22 SHARK

SHRIMP

WATER

Here are more books to read about oceans:
Animals of the Oceans (Animals by Habitat)
by Stephen Savage
Raintree/Steck Vaughn

Diving into Oceans (Ranger Rick's
Naturescope Guides)
McGraw Hill

A B Sea
by Bobbie Kalman
Crabtree Publishers

To learn more about oceans, check out these
Web sites:
http://www.oceanicresearch.org
http://www.fi.edu/oceans/oceans.html

Index

Word Count: 112

Note to Librarians, Teachers, and Parents

PowerKids Readers (Nature Books) are specially designed to help emergent and beginning readers build their skills in reading for information. Simple vocabulary and concepts are paired with photographs of real kids in real-life situations or stunning, detailed images from the natural world around them. Readers will respond to written language by linking meaning with their own everyday experiences and observations. Sentences are short and simple, employing a basic vocabulary of sight words, as well as new words that describe objects or processes that take place in the natural world. Large type, clean design, and photographs corresponding directly to the text all help children to decipher meaning. Features such as a contents page, picture glossary, and index help children get the most out of PowerKids Readers. They also introduce children to the basic elements of a book, which they will encounter in their future reading experiences. Lists of related books and Web sites encourage kids to explore other sources and to continue the process of learning.